Anonymous

Rules and Orders of Practice of the Superior Court, Lower Canada

SALZWASSER
VERLAG

Anonymous

Rules and Orders of Practice of the Superior Court, Lower Canada

Reprint of the original.

1st Edition 2023 | ISBN: 978-3-37514-642-9

Verlag (Publisher): Salzwasser Verlag GmbH, Zeilweg 44, 60439 Frankfurt, Deutschland
Vertretungsberechtigt (Authorized to represent): E. Roepke, Zeilweg 44, 60439 Frankfurt, Deutschland
Druck (Print): Books on Demand GmbH, In de Tarpen 42, 22848 Norderstedt, Deutschland

RULES

AND

ORDERS OF PRACTICE

OF THE

SUPERIOR COURT,

LOWER CANADA.

———◆———

QUEBEC:
PRINTED BY J. T. BROUSSEAU, 7, BUADE STREET, UPPER TOWN.

1858.

LOWER CANADA.

SUPERIOR COURT.

It is Ordered—That from henceforth, all previous Rules of Practice be rescinded, and that the following RULES AND ORDERS OF PRACTICE be, and the same are hereby established and declared to be the Rules and Orders of Practice of this Court:—

CHAPTER I.

Of the Officers of the Court.

I.

That the Queen's Counsel, and Barristers, who practice in this Court, do appear, when in Court, habited in black, and in such robes and bands as are worn by the Queen's Counsel and Barristers in Westminster Hall, as heretofore hath been used, and that no Queen's Counsel, or Barrister, be heard in any cause who is not so habited.

II.

That every Attorney practising in this Court, do file, in writing, in the Office of the Prothonotary, an election of his domicile, as such Attorney, at some place within a Mile of the Court House at the place where he practises; and that in default of his so doing, he shall be considered to have elected his domicile as such Attorney, for all intents and purposes, in the Office of the Prothonotary at such place.

XVIII.

That all services on the Attorney of any party be made between the hours of Nine, A. M., and SIX, P. M., from the Twenty-first of March to the Twenty-first of September; and between the hours of Nine, A. M., and Five P. M., during the remainder of the year.

That every service of process and other service on any party to a suit be made between the hours of Eight in the Forenoon and the hour of Seven in the Afternoon.

CHAPTER V.

Of Appearances—and of Bail.

XIX.

That of every appearance which shall be filed for a Defendant, a duplicate or certified copy shall be served during the same day upon the Plaintiff's Attorney.

XX.

That no change of Attornies shall in any case be allowed without leave of Court, or of a Judge in Vacation.

XXI.

That an Attorney who shall appear for any person shall not, without leave of Court, or of a Judge in vacation, be permitted to withdraw from the suit in which he shall have so appeared.

XXII.

That in every suit in which a party shall cease to be represented by Attorney he may be compelled, by Rule of Court, to substitute an Attorney or an appearance· in person; and in default of a Plaintiff so doing, his action shall be dismissed with costs, *sauf à se pourvoir*—in default of a Defendant so doing it shall be competent for the Plaintiff to proceed *exparte*.

XXIII.

That no surrender of any Defendant, by himself or by his Bail, shall be valid or effectual, or allowed as such,

III.

That the Prothonotary of this Court do appear, when in Court, habited in black and in such robes and bands as are worn by the Prothonotary in Westminster Hall, as heretofore hath been used; that the Sheriff, when in Court, do appear, habited in black, with his robe, his wand of office and sword as heretofore hath been used; and that the Crier, when in Court, do appear habited in black and in such robe as is worn by that Officer in Westminster Hall.

IV.

That the Offices of the Prothonotary and of the Sheriff, be open on every Juridical day during Term, and also in the Districts of Quebec and Montreal, on every Monday being a Juridical day, from the hour of Eight in the Morning until the hour of Six in the afternoon; and in the Districts of Quebec and Montreal, during Vacation, Mondays excepted, from the hour of Nine in the Morning until the hour of Four in the Afternoon of every Juridical day, and in the Districts of Three Rivers, St. Francis, and Gaspé, during Vacation, from the hour of Nine in the Morning until Noon, and from the hour of Two to the hour of Four in the Afternoon.

V.

That the Sheriff, the Prothonotary and the Crier, do personally attend in Court, in their respective places, *de die in diem*, during each Term from the opening until the rising of the Court, and in like manner during all Sittings of the Court held in Vacation.

VI.

That no Barrister or Attorney, Prothonotary, Sheriff, Crier, Bailiff, or Sheriff's Officer, shall be bail or surety in any action or proceedings cognizable by this Court, or by any Judge thereof.

VII.

That all Orders and Rules for the conduct and regulation of the Sheriff in the execution of his duty, shall extend to the Coroner, in all cases in which such duty shall be executed by him.

CHAPTER II.

General Orders.

VIII.

That the Rules and Orders of Practice of this Court shall be fairly entered by the Prothonotary in a book to be by him kept for that purpose; and all decisions of this Court on points of practice, shall also be entered by the Prothonotary, when so directed by the Court, in another book to be by him kept for that purpose—to each of which books there shall be an index, and all Practitioners of this Court, shall, during office-hours, have access thereto, and therefrom be allowed to take extracts and copies *gratis.*

IX.

That all Writs and other pratical Forms, which are or shall be settled by this Court, shall in like manner be fairly entered by the Prothonotary in a Register to be by him kept for that purpose, to which there shall be an index, and all Practitioners of this Court shall at all times, during office-hours, have access thereto, and therefrom be allowed to take extracts and copies *gratis.*

X.

That every wilful breach of an Order or Rule of Practice of this Court (for which no fine or other specific punishment is provided in the body of such Rule or Order) shall be considered a comtempt of Court, and punished accordingly.

XI.

That in computations of time no fractions of a day be allowed, nor shall any Sunday or binding holiday (*fête d'obligation*) be reckoned unless otherwise provided for by law.

XII.

That whenever any delay shall expire on a non Juridical day, such delay shall be enlarged to the next Juridical day.

XIII.

That no paper of any description shall be received by the Prothonotary, in any cause, unless the same be regularly docketted by mentioning the Title and Number of the cause, the general description of such paper, and the party fyling the same.

CHAPTER III.

Of Process ad Respondendum.

XIV.

That a Register of all and every process *ad respondendum* whatsoever, issued from this Court, specifying the names of the parties, the amount demanded, the cause of action, and the return day of each process respectively, shall be kept by the Prothonotary, to which all persons, during office-hours, shall have access *gratis*.

XV.

That no process *ad respondendum* of any description shall issue, until an appearance for the party requiring such process, and a *Præcipe*, for the same, be filed in the Office of the Prothonotary.

XVI.

That no process *ad respondendum*, founded upon affidavit, shall issue in any suit until the affidavit upon which such process is founded be filed by the Plaintiff in the Office of the Prothonotary.

CHAPTER IV.

Of Certificates of Service, &c.

XVII.

That every affidavit or Certificate of Service shall particularly describe the manner, place and time of service, in letters, and also the distance, from the place of service, to the Court House, at which the party is required to appear.

unless such surrender be made in open Court, or before
one of the Judges of this Court in Vacation, nor unless the
Court or such Judge before whom such surrender shall be
made, shall have made an entry or minute of such surrender,
and shall have committed such Defendant thereupon to the
custody of the Sheriff in discharge of such bail; and in
every case of surrender made before any Judge of the
Court, the Minute of such surrender shall forthwith be
returned into the office of the Prothonotary, and there be
filed of Record, in the suit to which such minute shall
relate, and a copy of such minute shall, by the Prothonotary,
be delivered with such Defendant to the said Sheriff.

CHAPTER VI.

Of Exhibits and communication of Papers.

XXIV.

That all Paper-writings, whereon any Declaration or
other Pleading is founded, or duly certified copies of such
papers, shall, with lists thereof, be filed together with such
Declaration or other pleading respectively, and not afterwards, unless by the special permission of the Court; and
that all other paper-writings which any party shall see fit
to produce in evidence, together with the originals of all
actes sous seing privé, copies of which shall have been filed
as hereinbefore directed, shall be exhibited and filed with
lists thereof, before the *Enquête* of the party producing the
same be closed.

XXV.

That every List of Exhibits shall be an index to all the
Exhibits therewith filed, by number, title, date and description, under the signature of the Attorney or party filing
such Exhibits, and any Exhibit, which shall not be so
mentioned in such list, shall not be received.

XXVI.

That all delays to plead shall be reckoned from the day
on which the Exhibits, in support of the Pleading to be
answered, shall have been filed.

XXVII.

That all parties to a suit shall be entitled to communication of all Exhibits and other paper-writings, filed in such suit, at the office of the Prothonotary.

XXVIII.

That of all Exhibits or other paper-writings in any cause, being copies of *actes authentiques* or of papers *sous seing privé*, communication shall be given on the receipt of the party indorsed, dated and signed upon the List of Exhibits, and such party shall be entitled to retain such copies in communication during forty-eight hours ; it being expressly provided that no original paper-writing shall be removed from the Office of the Prothonotary for any cause whatsoever.

XXIX.

That no Exhibit, in any cause shall be withdrawn pending such cause, or within a year and a day from the final Judgment in such cause, without an order of the Court or of a Judge in Vacation ; and before such Exhibit or other paper-writing be withdrawn, a copy thereof (except of authentic Instruments) certified by the Prothonotary, shall be filed of record, unless otherwise ordered by the Court or Judge.

CHAPTER VII.

Of Pleadings.

XXX.

That whenever the particulars of any *demande* shall not be disclosed by the Declaration, and no Bill of particulars shall be therewith filed, no proceedings shall be had upon such Declaration, but the same shall, upon the Motion of the adverse party, be rejected, and thereupon the action of the Plaintiff be dismissed, unless it be otherwise ordered by the Court upon sufficient cause shewn.

XXXI.

That of every pleading filed a certified copy shall be served upon the adverse party, and, until such service shall have been made, the pleading shall not be held to have been filed.

XXXII.

That no *exception déclinatoire, péremptoire à la forme* or *dilatoire* be received unless the party offering such exception shall therewith deposit in the hands of the Prothonotary the sum of Two Pounds One Shilling and Eightpence for every such exception, to answer the Costs of the adverse party, if such exception be dismissed or withdrawn, in the proportion of Eleven Shillings and Eightpence to the Prothonotary, and One Pound Ten Shillings to the Attorney.

XXXIII.

That upon every *exception déclinatoire, péremptoire à la forme* or *dilatoire* the plaintiff may move for hearing, without an answer; it being expressly provided that every Plaintiff, so moving shall thereby, for the purpose of such hearing, be held to confess the allegations contained in such exception.

XXXIV.

That in every case in which an *exception déclinatoire, dilatoire* or *péremptoire à la forme* shall be filed, the delay to plead to the merits shall be computed from the day on which such exception shall have been disposed of.

XXXV.

That with every *défense au fonds en droit* shall be filed a notice assigning all the grounds of such *défense au fonds en droit;* it being expressly ordered that no party shall be permitted to urge any ground, in support of a *défense au fonds en droit,* not so set forth and particularised in such notice.

CHAPTER VIII.

Of Incidental Cross Demands, Interventions and Evocations.

XXXVI.

That every Incidental cross demand shall be filed at the same time with the plea to the action; and no such Incidental Cross demand shall be afterwards received.

XXXVII.

That every Incidental Cross Demand shall be deemed a distinct action, and shall not delay the proceedings of the Plaintiff.

XXXVIII.

That every cause brought by evocation before this Court, and in which the Plaintiff shall think fit to file another Declaration, such Plaintiff shall, within Eight days from the allowance of such evocation, file such other Declaration.

XXXIX.

That the Rules, Orders and delays prescribed by Law, or by this Court, with respect to the pleadings upon Demands in chief, shall in all things apply to and be the Rules, Orders and delays, with respect to all pleadings upon Incidental Demands, Interventions and causes brought before the Court by evocation.

CHAPTER IX.

Of Enquêtes.

XL.

That there shall be kept, in the office of the Prothonotary, a Roll, to be called the *Roll des Enquêtes,* upon which shall be inscribed all causes set down for the adduction of proof.

XLI.

That no proof shall be adduced in any contested cause unless two days in Term, or eight days in Vacation, shall have intervened between the notice of such inscription and the day appointed for the making of proof.

XLII.

That as soon as the issues of fact shall be perfected in any cause in which no issue of law hath been raised, or, if raised, hath been disposed of, either party may inscribe the cause upon the *Roll des Enquêtes.*

XLIII.

That if, on the day appointed for adducing proof, the party bound to proceed shall not appear, or appearing shall not proceed, or shew legal cause for not proceeding, his *Enquête* shall, upon the application of the adverse party, be declared closed, and a day, if necessary, shall be fixed for the *Enquête* of such adverse party upon his application to that effect.

XLIV.

That a witness shall be examined by one Counsel and no more, and cross-examined by one Counsel and no more.

XLV.

That any cause inscribed on the *Roll des Enquêtes* shall remain thereon, until the *Enquête* in such cause shall have been declared closed, and shall be held to be continued from day to day without any special application to that effect. Provided always that if more than one day shall elapse without any proceeding or application in such cause, and without the same being specially continued to a day certain, no proceeding or application shall thereafter be taken or received without notice of at least one day to the adverse party.

XLVI.

That all interrogatories to be annexed to any order or *Commission, in the nature of a Commission Rogatoire,* unless settled by consent, shall be allowed by one of the Judges.

XLVII.

That if any such order or Commission shall not be returned on the day appointed for such return, (if such there be) or within a reasonable time after the issuing thereof, (if such order or Commission be returnable without delay) it shall be competent for the parties to proceed in such cause, as if no order or Commission had issued, unless good cause to the contrary be shewn, on Motion to that effect.

XLVIII.

That either party shall, at any time, have a right, by application to the Court in Term, or to a Judge in Vacation, to cause the return to any order or commission to be opened, unless good cause to the contrary be shewn; but the return to an order or Commission, issued at the instance of the Defendant, shall not be opened until the Plaintiff's *Enquête* be closed.

XLIX.

That in all cases in which the service of a Rule for *serment décisoire* or for *faits et articles* shall be made within the distance of five leagues from the Court House, there shall be one intermediate Juridical day between the day of service and the day of return, and when beyond that distance, one intermediate Juridical day as above, and also one intermediate Juridical day for every five leagues of distance.

CHAPTER X.

Of the Inscription of Causes for Hearing.

L.

That there be kept in the office of the Prothonotary a Roll, to be called the *Roll de droit*, upon which shall be inscribed all causes for hearing upon any issue of law, or upon the merits, or other matter.

LI.

That no contested cause shall be heard upon any Inscription on the *Roll de droit* unless two Juridical days shall have intervened between the Inscription and the day appointed for the hearing.

LII.

That so soon as any issue of Law is perfected either party may inscribe the cause on the *Roll de droit* for hearing on such issue; and if, on the day appointed for the hearing, the party by whom such law issue hath been raised shall not appear, and his adversary shall appear, the pleading whereby the same hath been raised shall be dismissed with costs. If neither party be present the Inscription shall be discharged.

LIII.

That so soon as the *Enquête* upon any preliminary exception shall be closed, either party may inscribe the same upon the *Roll de droit*, for hearing on the merits of such exception, and if on the day appointed for the hearing thereof, the party Excipient shall not appear, his exception shall on the application of the adverse party be dismissed with costs. If neither party appear, the Inscription shall be discharged.

LIV.

That as soon as the *Enquête* in any contested cause shall be closed, either party may inscribe such cause on the *Roll de droit* for hearing on the merits, and if, on the day appointed for the hearing thereof, the Plaintiff shall not appear, his action shall on the application of the adverse party be dismissed with costs. If neither party appear, the Inscription shall be discharged.

CHAPTER XI.

Of Motions.

LV.

That no motion be received or heard unless previous notice thereof, of at least one day, be given to the adverse party, excepting the Motions whereupon side bar Rules may be obtained, and those hereinafter specially mentioned.

LVI.

That the parties shall not be heard on any Rule unless one day shall have intervened between the service of such Rule and the day appointed for the hearing thereof.

LVII.

That every Motion founded on special matter shall contain the grounds on which such Motion is made, and no party shall be permitted to urge any ground in support of a Motion not set forth in such Motion.

LVIII.

That the following Motions being Motions of course, may be made and filed in the Office of the Prothonotary, and be by him received, and Rules entered thereon, in the same manner as if made in open Court :—

1. For the Sheriff to return a Writ—*Nisi*.
2. For Particulars—*Nisi*.
3. For security for Costs, the Plaintiff being a person without that part of the Province, heretofore Lower Canada, and stated so to be, in the Declaration—*Nisi*.
4. To give security for Costs—*Nisi*.
5. For a Jury Trial—*Nisi*.
6. To strike a cause from the *Roll de droit* or *Roll des Enquêtes*—*Nisi*.
7. For a reference to *experts*—*Nisi*.
8. To set aside or confirm a Report—*Nisi*.
9. To pay money into Court—*Nisi*.
10. To file a Retraxit—*Nisi*.
11. To dismiss for want of proceedings—*Nisi*.
12. To discontinue on payment of Costs—*Nisi*.
13. For *acte* to party that he does not contest an Opposition.
14. For a Rule on Defendant for *main levée* on such Opposition—*Nisi*.
15. To homologate a report of Distribution—*Nisi*.
16. For the Sheriff to bring in the body—*Nisi*.

LIX.

That the following Motions may be made and adjudicated upon without notice to the adverse party :—

1. For judgment pursuant to confession, or to a verdict of Jury.
2. To defer or refer the *serment décisoire*.
3. For *faits et articles*.
4. To obtain *acte* of the Court.

LX.

That a party intending to produce any Affidavit, or other paper-writing in support of any Motion or Rule, shall with the notice of such motion, or copy of such rule, serve on the opposite party copies of the Affidavits, or other paper-writings intended to be produced, and in default of his so doing, the opposite party shall be entitled to delay, until the next day, to take communication of such papers.

LXI.

That the validity of every Report of *Experts*, or Award of Arbitrators shall be decided upon a motion, or upon a Rule *nisi* to homologate the Report, or to set the Report aside, as the case may be.

LXII.

That every application for security for costs shall be made within four days from the appearance of the party making such application.

LXIII.

That all costs to which, in any case, a party is entitled upon a Motion in any way, be asked for at the time at which such Motion is made and heard, and not afterwards.

CHAPTER XII.

Of Trials by Jury.

LXIV.

That in every cause wherein a Trial by Jury may by law be had, the party desiring such trial shall declare his option, either by his declaration or plea, or by Motion to be made within four days after the issue is perfected; and after the said four days, either party may move for the appointment of a day for trial and the issuing of a *Venire facias.*

LXV.

That with every such Motion the party shall be bound to deposit, in the hands of the Prothonotary, the sum of Five Pounds, Six Shillings and Eight pence, to be distributed as follows :—

To the Prothonotary for striking the Jury, for the Writ of *Venire facias,* for calling and swearing the Jury, and for recording the Verdict, Twenty Shillings.

To the Sheriff for his services according to the Tariff, Twenty Shillings.

To the Crier, Six Shillings and Eigth pence.

And for the Jurors the sum of Three Pounds, the amount allowed by Law.

LXVI.

That the Sheriff shall not be bound to summon such Jury until a sum of money be placed in his hands, sufficient to pay the costs of summoning such Jury.

LXVII.

That any difference respecting the amount of the sum to be so deposited be determined by one of the Judges.

LXVIII.

That if the sum so deposited be more than sufficient to pay such costs, the surplus shall be returned to the party who deposited the same, and if it be insufficient, the balance shall be paid to the Sheriff before the Jury shall be sworn.

LXIX.

That the striking of the Jury shall take place in the Office of the Prothonotary.

LXX.

That the party who obtains an order for a *Venire facias* shall give a notice to the opposite party, of at least one day, of the time appointed for the striking of the Jury, but the

want of such notice shall not prevent the striking of the
Jury, if the party entitled to notice do not object to such
want of notice.

LXXI.

That if the Attorney of either of the parties make default
to appear before the Prothonotary at the time appointed
for the striking of the Jury, or appearing, shall refuse to
strike out from the list of Jurors, in such cause, the names
of twelve, or of any lesser number of such Jurors, the
Prothonotary, in the absence, or on the refusal of such
Attorney, shall strike out of the said List of Jurors, twelve
on behalf of the party of such Attorney, in the manner
directed by law, or such lesser number as the Attorney shall
refuse or neglect to strike out.

LXXII.

That in every case in which a Trial by Jury shall be
ordered, two days at least before the day appointed for
such trial, *Factums* or Paper Books containing a statement
of the facts to be proved and of the Authorities in support
of the demand and of the defence, be delivered by the
parties respectively, sealed up, to the Prothonotary to be
by him forthwith delivered to the Judge whose duty it
may be to preside at the trial of such case.

LXXIII.

That so soon as the *Venire facias* shall be returned, the
parties shall be called, and if neither party shall appear,
the Jury shall be forthwith discharged; but if the Plaintiff
shall appear and the Defendant, being so called, shall not
appear, the default of such Defendant shall be recorded,
and thereupon the evidence of the plaintiff shall be heard
Exparte, the verdict of the Jury taken thereon, and judgment entered as to Law and Justice shall appertain. And
if the Defendant being so called shall appear, and the
Plaintiff, being called, shall not appear, the default of such
Plaintiff shall be recorded and Judgment of *non*-suit
thereupon entered in due course, dismissing such Plaintiff,
sauf à se pourvoir, with costs to the Defendant.

LXXIV.

That in every case in which a Jury shall be sworn, and
the Plaintiff in such cause shall choose, at any time before

the verdict of such Jury shall be given, to become *non*-suit, and for that purpose shall withdraw from the Court, such Plaintiff shall be called, and not appearing, the default of such Plaintiff shall be recorded, and Judgment of *non*-suit shall thereupon be entered in due course, dismissing such Plaintiff *sauf à se pourvoir* with costs to the Defendant.

LXXV.

That a Motion for a Judgment upon a verdict shall not be made until after the expiration of four days in term, from the day on which such verdict shall be recorded.

LXXVI.

That every Motion for a new Trial, after verdict, be made on or before the fourth day in term next after the day on which such verdict shall be recorded.

LXXVII.

That every Motion in arrest of Judgment after Verdict, be made on or before the expiration of the fourth day in Term, next after the day on which such verdict shall be recorded ; except when a motion for a new Trial shall have been made, in which case such Motion in arrest of Judgment shall be made on the second day next after the day on which such Motion for a new trial, shall have been disposed of.

CHAPTER XIII.

Oppositions and Executions.

LXXVIII.

That no Writ of Execution shall issue until a *Præcipe* for such Writ be filed in the Office of the Prothonotary, and that every such Writ be indorsed or signed by the Attorney or person by whom such Writ shall be so sued out.

LXXIX.

That a Register of all Writs of Execution issued from this Court, specifying the description of each Writ, the parties to the cause in which it issues, the number of such cause, the name of the Attorney or person by whom such Writ shall be sued out, the amount to be levied by virtue thereof, the cause of action, the date of the Judgment on which such Writ shall be founded, the day on which such Writ shall issue, and the return day thereof, be made and kept by the Prothonotary in his Office, to which all persons shall at all times, during office hours, have access *gratis*.

LXXX.

That to all Oppositions *afin d'annuller*, *afin de charge* or *afin de distraire*, there shall be annexed an affidavit in the form following :—

" *Lower Canada,* }
　District of }　　　　IN THE SUPERIOR COURT.

　　　　　　　　　　　　　　　　　　　PLAINTIFF ;

　　　　　　　　vs.

　　　　　　　　　　　　　　　　　　　DEFENDANT ;

A. B., of　　　　　　　　　　　　　　being duly sworn, doth depose and say that the facts articulated and set forth in the annexed opposition *afin d*　　　　, and each and every of them, is and are true ; and that the said opposition is not made with any intent unjustly to retard or delay the sale of the whole, or any part of the (*moveable* or *immoveable*) property, seized by virtue of the Writ or Writs of Execution in this cause issued, but that the same is made in good faith for the sole purpose of obtaining justice.

" *Sworn before me, at* ⎞
　　　　　, this ⎟
　　　　day of ⎟
　One thousand ⎟
Eight hundred and ⎟
　　　　　　" ⎠

LXXXI.

And any Opposition to which an affidavit in form aforesaid shall not be annexed, shall not delay the Execution of any Writ of *Fieri Facias* or *Venditioni Exponas* issued in any cause ; and notwithstanding the service or filing of any such Opposition, the Sheriff shall in such cause, proceed to the due execution of such Writ in like manner as if no Opposition had been served or filed. It being nevertheless provided that all such Oppositions shall be returned into this Court with such Writ .

LXXXII.

That in all cases of Opposition *afin de distraire* or *afin de charge,* founded upon Title, it shall not be necessary to annex to such Oppositions any affidavit in support of the same.

LXXXIII.

That every Opposition *afin de conserver* be filed, on or before the sixth day next after the return day mentioned in the Writ of Execution, under which the monies claimed by such Opposition shall have been levied ; provided that, in case the said Writ be returned into the Office of the Prothonotary on a day subsequent to the said return day, such Opposition may be filed on or before the sixth day next after the day on which such Execution shall be so actually returned. And no Opposition shall be afterwards received, unless upon sufficient cause shewn, and upon such Terms as the Court shall adjudge.

LXXXIV.

That in every case wherein the Plaintiff shall declare that he does not intend to contest an Opposition *afin d'annuller, afin de distraire* or *afin de charge,* the Opposant shall be entitled to Judgment of *main levée,* without proof : provided that the Defendant, upon the service of a Rule *Nisi* to that effect, shall not shew cause to the contrary, or declare that he intends to contest such Opposition.

LXXXV.

That the Rules, Orders and delays, prescribed by law or by this Court, with respect to pleadings, *Enquêtes* and hearings upon demands in chief, shall be the Rules, Orders and delays, with respect to all pleadings, *Enquêtes* and hearings upon Oppositions of every description.

LXXXVI.

That a Register of all Writs of Execution, and of all Oppositions filed in the Office of the Sheriff, containing a full description of such Writs and Oppositions, and of all proceedings and matters relating thereto, be made and kept by the said Sheriff in his Office, to which all persons shall, at all times during office hours, have access *gratis.*

LXXXVII.

That any Opposition, made without the ministry of an Attorney of this Court, which shall not contain an election of Domicile on the part of the Opposant, at some dwelling house within one mile from the Court House, shall not be received or filed.

LXXXVIII.

That every Opposition shall contain the *Moyens* upon which the same is founded, and that no other *Moyens d'Opposition* shall thereafter be received or filed.

LXXXIX.

That with every Opposition *afin de conserver*, shall be filed all the Exhibits in support thereof, with a List of such Exhibits.

XC.

That within twelve days after the return day of any Writ of Execution, and after the Sheriff's return thereto, certifying that there are monies in his hands subject to the Order of the Court, the Prothonotary shall prepare and file a Report of Distribution.

XCI.

That the Prothonotary shall prepare a List of all such Reports filed, and that such List shall be posted up in some conspicuous place in the Office of the Prothonotary.

XCII.

That any party intending to contest such Report shall file his Contestation at the Office of the Prothonotary, on or before the expiration of Eight days next after the filing of such Report; provided always, that if the Report of Distribution be filed on any day other than a Monday, the delay for filing the Contestation, shall be computed from the Monday next following the day on which such Report shall have been filed.

XCIII.

That immediately after the delay for filing such Contestation shall have expired, if no Contestation has been filed, the Plaintiff, may move that the said Report be homologated with Costs : and if the Plaintiff omit to make such motion, on the juridical day, next following the expiration of the delay for the filing of contestations, any other party collocated may make such Motion.

XCIV.

That the Rule obtained for the homologation of such Report shall not be served on the parties, but that the same shall be posted in the Prothonotary's Office, as heretofore, at least four days.

XCV.

That in every case in which a Report of Distribution shall be made and filed by the Prothonotary, and a Contestation of such Report or of any Claim or Opposition on which such Report shall be founded, shall be made and filed, such Report, upon Motion to be made as hereinafter mentioned, shall be confirmed and homologated, as to all uncontested claims and Oppositions which shall precede in rank the Claim or Opposition which, by such Contestation, shall be contested, and as to all other uncontested Claims or Oppositions (if any there shall be) which cannot be affected by such Contestation ; and Judgment according to such Report, in so far as the same shall be so confirmed and homologated, shall be entered up and Recorded, unless cause to the contrary shall be shewn. It being hereby provided that the Rule for such partial homologation shall not be served upon the parties, but that the same be publicly affixed in the Office of the Prothonotary at least four days. And that the Plaintiff shall have an exclusive right to move for the partial homologation of such report during the juridical day next following the expiration of the delay for the filing of Contestations ; and if the Plaintiff omit to move for the partial homologation of the report, within the said juridical day, immediately thereafter, any party collocated may move for such partial homologation.

XCVI.

That none of the delays hereinbefore mentioned with respect to Oppositions *afin de conserver*, and Reports of

Collocation and Distribution, shall be held to run during the month of August.

CHAPTER XIV.

XCVII.

That any party requiring a notice of an application for a Confirmation of Title shall demand the same by a *Prœcipe*.

CHAPTER XV.

Saisie Arrêt after Judgment.

XCVIII.

That any party intending to contest the Declaration of a *Tiers Saisi*, shall file his Contestation within Eight days from the making of the Declaration of the *Tiers saisi*, if the Attachment be an Attachment after Judgment; and if the Attachment be an Attachment before Judgment, then within Eight days from the rendering of the Judgment in the original Cause.

XCIX.

That the Rules, Orders and delays prescribed by law or by this Court with respect to Pleadings, *Enquêtes*, and hearings upon Demands in chief, shall be the Rules, Orders and delays with respect to all Pleadings, *Enquêtes*, and hearings upon the Contestation of the Declaration of any *Tiers saisi*.

CHAPTER XVI.

Inscriptions en faux.

C.

A party desirous of Inscribing *en faux* against an Exhibit filed shall, by Motion addressed to the Court, pray leave so to do.

CI.

The motion for leave to Inscribe *en faux* shall be signed by the party in whose name it is made, or by an Attorney specially authorised so to do, and an authenticated copy of the Power of Attorney given shall be filed with the said Motion.

CII.

The party filing such Exhibit shall, within a delay to be prescribed by the Court, on Motion of the Plaintiff *en faux*, declare in writing whether he intend to avail himself of such Exhibit in support of the allegations set forth in his pleading.

CIII.

Should the party filing such Exhibit omit to make such Declaration in writing, signed by himself, or by his Attorney *ad lites*, within the time prescribed, the said Exhibit shall, by Order of the Court, on the Motion of the Plaintiff *en faux*, be taken off the files of the Court, and shall thereafter be held and considered, to all intents and purposes, to have been withdrawn by the party who filed the same.

CIV.

If the Defendant *en faux* declare that he does not intend to avail himself of such Exhibit in support of his allegations, the said Exhibit shall be taken off the files of the Court, and shall be held and considered, to all intents and purposes, to have been withdrawn by the party who files the same.

CV.

If the Defendant *en faux* declare his intention to avail himself of such Exhibit for the purposes aforesaid, he shall file the *minute* thereof, if there be a *minute*, in the Office of the Prothonotary, within such time as shall be prescribed by the Court, and in default of so doing, the said Exhibit shall, on Motion of the Plaintiff *en faux*, be taken off the files of the Court, and held and considered, to all intents and purposes, to have been withdrawn by the party who filed the same.

CVI.

Two days after the Plaintiff *en faux* shall have been notified of the filing of the said *minute* at the Office of the said Prothonotary, the said Plaintiff shall file, under his signature or that of his Attorney *ad lites*, his Inscription *en faux*, containing all the *Moyens de faux*, a copy whereof, shall be served on the Attorney of the adverse party.

CVII.

If the said Plaintiff omit so to do, the leave granted to him to Inscribe *en faux* shall, on Motion of the adverse party, be set aside, and the Plaintiff on the original demand allowed to proceed as if leave to Inscribe *en faux* had not been granted.

CVIII.

When the *Moyens de faux* are filed, the Defendant *en faux* may move that the said *Moyens* be declared irrelevant and inadmissible, on which Motion it shall be competent to the Court, if it reject the same, to declare the *Moyens de faux* revelant and admissible, and to Order the Defendant *en faux* to file his Plea thereto within a given delay, to be computed from the day of the making of the *Procès Verbal* next hereinafter mentioned.

CIX.

That immediately after the rendering of the said Judgment declaring the *Moyens de faux* relevant and admissible, the Plaintiff or Defendant *en faux* may move that a *Procès Verbal*, descriptive of the Exhibit filed, be made in the presence of the adverse party, or his Attorney *ad lites*.

CX.

If the Defendant *en faux* omit to file his Plea, as ordered, the Plaintiff *en faux* shall be allowed to proceed *Exparte*.

CXI.

The Plaintiff *en faux* may, within two days from the day of the filing of such Plea, file a special answer thereto, if he think fit.

CXII.

Either party may inscribe the cause on the *Roll d'Enquête* for the adduction of evidence.

CXIII.

The *Enquête* being closed, either party may inscribe the cause for final hearing.

CXIV.

The cause being Inscribed on the *Roll d'Enquête*, and subsequently on the *Roll de droit*, the proceedings thereon shall be regulated by the Orders and Rules of Practice of this Court.

QUEBEC, 17th December, 1850.

(Signed,)　　EDWD. BOWEN, CHIEF JUSTICE, S. C.,
CHS. D. DAY, J. S. C.,
G. VANFELSON, J. S. C.,
CHARLES MONDELET, J. S. C.,
E. BACQUET, J. S. C.,
J. DUVAL, J. S. C.,
W. C. MEREDITH, J. S. C.

LOWER CANADA.

SUPERIOR COURT.

It is Ordered—That the following additional Rules of Practice be observed in the Districts of Three Rivers, St. Francis and Gaspe, anything in the General Rules and Orders of Practice of this Court to the contrary notwithstanding :

I.

That no contested cause shall be heard upon any inscription on the *Roll de droit* unless one juridical day shall have intervened between the Inscription and the day appointed for the hearing.

II.

That every Opposition *afin de conserver* be filed on or before the second day next after the return day mentioned in the Writ of Execution under which the monies claimed by such Opposition shall have been levied. Provided that in case the said Writ bo returned in the Office of the Prothonotary on a day subsequent to the said return day such Opposition may be filed on or before the second day next after the day on which such execution shall be so actually returned. And no Opposition shall be afterwards received, unless upon sufficient cause shown and upon such terms as the Court shall adjudge.

III.

That within four days after the return day of any Writ of execution, and after the Sheriff's return thereof, certifying that there are monies in his hands subject to the order of the Court, the Prothonotary shall prepare and file a Report of distribution or of collocation.

IV.

That any party intending to contest such Report shall file his Contestation (after a copy thereof has been served on the interested party) at the office of the Prothonotary on or before the expiration of two days next after the filing of such Report.

V.

That the Rule obtained for the homologation of any Report or partial Report shall not be served on the parties but that the same shall be posted up by a Bailiff of the Court in the Prothonotary's Office, at least one juridical day.

QUEBEC, 17th December, 1850.

(Signed,) EDWD. BOWEN, CHIEF JUSTICE S. C.,
D. MONDELET, J. S. C.,
CHS. D. DAY, J. S. C.,
J. SMITH, J. S. C.,
G. VANFELSON, J. S. C.,
CHARLES MONDELET, J. S. C.,
E. BACQUET, J. S. C.,
J. DUVAL, J. S. C.,
W. C. MEREDITH, J. S. C.

LOWER CANADA.

—

SUPERIOR COURT.

30th June, 1852.

It is Ordered.—That the several Rules of Practice now in force and ordered to be observed in the Districts of Three Rivers, St. Francis and Gaspé, homologated and bearing date at Quebec, 17th December 1850, be extended to and observed in the Districts of Ottawa and Kamouraska.

EDWD. BOWEN, Ch. Justice.
D. MONDELET, J. S. C.
J. SMITH,
CHARLES MONDELET, J. S. C.
G. VANFELSON, J. S. C.
J. DUVAL, J.
W. C. MEREDITH, J. S. C.

Registered at Quebec, this twenty-ninth day of November, one thousand eight hundred and fifty-two.

BURROUGHS & FISET, P. S. C.

LOWER CANADA.

SUPERIOR COURT.

4th January, 1854.

ORDERED—That the following RULES AND ORDERS OF PRACTICE be observed in this Court.

That immediately after the delay for filing a Contestation to a Report of Distribution shall have expired, if no Contestation has been filed, the Plaintiff may give notice that he will move on the first Juridical day of the ensuing Term, that the said Report be homologated with costs; and if the Plaintiff omit to give such notice on the Juridical day next following the expiration of the delay for the filing of Contestations, any other party collocated may give such notice.

That the said notice shall not be served on the parties; but that the same shall be posted in the Prothonotary's Office, at least four days.

That every Demurrer to a Plea or Special Answer, shall contain an Assignment of the causes on which that Demurrer is founded.

That a party served with a Rule to Answer Interrogatories upon *Faits et Articles*, shall give his answers before the closing of the *Enquête* of the party who has obtained the Rule; and that no Answers shall be afterwards received, except by leave of the Court obtained on a special application for the same.

That a motion for leave to inscribe *en faux* against an Exhibit filed, shall be made within four days of the filing of the Exhibit, and not afterwards, unless allowed on special application for the same.

That it shall be lawful for a Defendant, by leave of a Judge of this Court, to pay into Court the sum of money which such Defendant acknowledges to owe to the Plaintiff, and thereupon, unless the Plaintiff shall accept thereof in full discharge of his suit, the said sum shall be struck out of the Declaration and paid out of Court to the Plaintiff; and upon the trial of the issue, the Plaintiff shall not be allowed to give evidence for the sum so acknowledged to be due.

EDWD. BOWEN, Ch. Justice.
CHARLES MONDELET, J. S. C.
CHAS. D. DAY, J. S. C.
J. DUVAL, J.
W. C MEREDITH, J. S. C.
ED. CARON, J. C. S.

Registered at Quebec, this fourth day of January, one thousand eight hundred and fifty-four.

BURROUGHS & FISET,
P. S. C.

SUPERIOR COURT.

TABLE OF FEES,

OF 1850.

Abrogated as to Fees of Attornies and Bailiffs by Tariff of June 1852.

LOWER CANADA.—SUPERIOR COURT.(*)

It is Ordered that the following Fees be allowed to the undermentioned Officers:—

TABLE I.

(*) Abrogated as to fees of Attornies and Bailiffs by Tariff of June 1852.

ACTIONS NOT CONTESTED.	CLASS I. In personal Actions if the matters in contest exceed £250, currency, and in Petitory actions.		CLASS II. In personal Actions if the matters in contest exceed £100, and do not exceed £250, cy., and in real and mixed actions, not specially provided for and also in actions en Reddition de compte, [pro socio.] ou en séparation de biens or en séparation de corps et de biens.		CLASS III. In personal Actions if the matters in contest do not exceed £100, cy., and in Actions en exhibition de titres and also under the Lessors and Lessees Act, 3 William IV., cap. L.	
	Plaintiff's Attorney. £ s. d	Defendant's Attorney. £ s. d.	Plaintiff's Attorney. £ s. d.	Defendant's Attorney. £ s. d.	Plaintiff's Attorney. £ s. d.	Defendant's Attorney. £ s. d.
If the action be settled after the taking out of the Writ, but before the return......	4 3 4		3 6 8		2 10 0	
If the action be settled after default recorded for want of appearance, or after foreclosure for want of a Plea, but before the opening of the Enquête, where an Enquête is necessary, and before the Inscription for Judgment where no Enquête is necessary; or if the action be settled before Plea to the Merits, when the Defendant has appeared and has not been foreclosed from pleading; or if the Defendant confess Judgment before pleading to the Merits or being foreclosed from pleading......	4 6 3		3 10 0		2 13 4	

	£ s d	£ s d	£ s d	£ s d	£ s d	£ s d
3. If the action be settled after the opening, but before the closing of the *Enquête*; or if the action be settled after the Inscription for Judgment, where no *Enquête* is necessary; or if Judgment be rendered on such Inscription......	6 5 0	5 0 0		5 0 0	3 15 0	
4. If the action be settled after *Enquête* closed or if Judgment be rendered in such action (after *Enquête*)......	8 6 8	6 13 4	2 0 0	6 13 4		1 13 4
5. If any of the above cases in which the Defendant may have appeared by Attorney—to Defendant's Attorney......		2 6 8				

Actions Contested.

	£ s d	£ s d	£ s d	£ s d	£ s d	£ s d
6. If the action be dismissed on any Plea other than a Plea to the Merits; or if the action be settled after Plea to the Merits, but before *Enquête*......	6 5 0	5 0 0	4 0 0	5 0 0	3 15 0	3 3 0
7. If the action be settled after the opening of the *Enquête*, but before final hearing on the Merits......	9 7 6	7 10 0	6 0 0	7 10 0	5 17 6	4 10 0
8. If the action be settled after final hearing on the Merits or if Judgment be rendered on such hearing.	12 10 0	10 0 0	8 0 0	10 0 0	7 16 0	6 6 0

ACTIONS en revendication for moveables to be classed according to the value of the thing claimed.

Hypothecary actions and actions for seigniorial dues, where the title of the Plaintiff as Seignior is not contested, are to be considered in respect of costs, as merely personal actions. In any case where there are more Defendants than one, and where they sever in their defence, to Plaintiff's Attorney, on each additional issue, one half of the sum which he would have received, had there been but one issue, the whole amount payable in equal proportions by the party or parties to each issue.

Additional Fees to TABLE I, when the cases may occur :—

	£	s.	d.
9. For the second and every additional Copy of the Plaintiff's Declaration	0	5	0
10. Affidavit to obtain *Capias ad Respondendum, Saisie Arrêt, Saisie Revendication* or *Saisie Gageri,* when affidavit required	0	10	0
On every *Exception déclinatoire, dilatoire* or *péremptoire à la forme,* and on every *défense au fonds en droit,* rejected,—			
11. To the Plaintiff's Attorney	1	10	0
12. To the Defendant's Attorney	1	3	4
If the Plaintiff be permitted to amend his Declaration, after fyling of an *Exception à la forme,*—			
13. To the Defendant's Attorney	1	15	0
If the Plaintiff be permitted to amend his Declaration after fyling of a *défense au fonds en droit,*			
14. To the Defendant's Attorney	2	6	8
On every *Exception dilatoire* maintained			
15. To the Defendant's Attorney'	2	6	8
16. To the Plaintiff's Attorney	1	3	4
For all proceedings on any application either before or after Judgment to liberate any person arrested for debt otherwise than by giving bail, or to obtain a *scellé* or the removal thereof,—			
17. If not contested—to each Attorney	1	3	4
18. If contested—to each Attorney	2	6	8
19. For all proceedings on any Petition, Motion or Rule not specially provided for, upon which Costs are ordered to be paid, to the party to whom Costs are awarded	0	11	8
Fee for Counsel at *Enquête* in any Contested Cause, this fee not to be allowed, unless an Appearance be fyled by the Counsel retained,—			
20. To each Attorney—If action of first class	2	6	8
21. Ditto If action of second class	1	15	0
22. Ditto If action of third class	1	6	8
23. This fee to be allowed in Actions tried by Jury in like manner as in other Actions.			
24. For all proceedings in an Action to have Judgment declared executory—same as in an Action *en Reprise d'Instance*			
For all proceedings in an Action *En Reprise d'Instance*—one-third of the fee that would be allowed on the original demand,			

		£	s	d
25.	On any rehearing ordered by the Court in a contested action,—			
26.	If action be of first class—to each Attorney	2	6	8
27.	If action be of second class—to each Attorney	1	15	0
28.	If action be of third class—to each Attorney	1	6	8
	For all proceedings on the sueing out of a Writ of Execution	0	6	8
29.	For all proceedings on the sueing out of a Writ of *Saisie Arrêt* after Judgment,—			
	If Declaration of *Tiers Saisi* be not contested—to the Plaintiff's Attorney	1	3	4
	If contested, the costs the same as in an original demand of the same class—to be determined by the amount of the Judgment against the *Tiers Saisi*,—			
	For all proceedings for a *folle Enchère* or for a Writ of Possession or for a *Contrainte par Corps*, except in the case hereinafter expressly provided for,—			
30.	To Attorney Moving	1	3	4
31.	To Attorney Shewing Cause	1	0	0
	For all proceedings for a *contrainte par corps* against any person for injuring real property under seizure,—			
32.	If not contested—To each Attorney	1	3	4
33.	If contested—To each Attorney	2	0	0
34.	For prosecuting to Judgment a Report of Distribution, not contested	2	10	0
	For all proceedings upon a contestation of a Report of Distribution which shall not be withdrawn before the Inscription for final hearing on the Merits—when the amount of the collocation contested is above £250,—			
35.	To the Attorney of the party contesting	4	3	4
36.	To the Attorney of the creditor claiming	3	6	8
	If the amount of the collocation contested exceed £100, and do not exceed £250,—			
37.	To the Attorney of the party contesting	3	6	8
38.	To the Attorney of the creditor claiming	2	10	0
	If the amount of the collocation contested exceed £50, and do not exceed £100,—			
39.	To the Attorney of the party contesting	2	10	0
40.	To the Attorney of the creditor claiming	2	0	0
	If the amount of the collocation contested exceed £25, and do not exceed £50,—			
41.	To the Attorney of the party contesting	1	16	8
42.	To the Attorney of the creditor claiming	1	6	8
	If the amount of the collocation contested do not exceed £25,—			

	£	s.	d.
43. To the Attorney of the party contesting...	1	10	0
44. To the Attorney of the creditor claiming...	1	3	4
If the contestation be withdrawn before the Inscription for hearing on the Merits—one half of the above fees according to the class;—			
For all proceedings after Judgment, ordering account to be rendered in any Action *en reddition de compte*— if the account be acquiesced in without *débats*,—	2	6	8
45. To each Attorney...			
If the account be contested, the costs to be the same as in a contested personal action, the class to be determined by the amount for which the *rendant compte* shall be held accountable, if the costs be payable by the *rendant compte*; and by the amount claimed by the *débats de compte* if the costs be payable by the *ayant compte*;—			
In Actions *en séparation de corps et de biens*—For all proceedings to liquidate the Matrimonial rights of the Plaintiff,—	2	6	8
46. If not contested—To each Attorney...	5	0	0
47. If contested—To each Attorney...	2	6	8
In Actions *en séparation de biens*—For all proceedings to liquidate the Matrimonial rights of the Plaintiff,—			
48. To the Plaintiff's Attorney...	1	3	4
49. For all proceedings to cause Curator to be appointed to *délaissement* in any hypothecary action...			
(And to Curator, £1 3s. 4d.)			

Inscriptions de faux.

	£	s.	d.
When cause settled after the *moyens de faux* are declared pertinent,—			
50. To the Attorney of the Plaintiff *en faux*...	2	6	8
51. To the Attorney of the Defendant *en faux*...	1	3	4
When cause settled after answer to the *moyens* and before *Enquête*,—			
52. To the Attorney of the Plaintiff *en faux*...	2	6	8
53. To the Attorney of the Defendant *en faux*...	1	13	4
When cause settled after *Enquête*,—			
54. To the Attorney of the Plaintiff *en faux*,—	3	10	0
55. To the Attorney of the Defendant *en faux*...	2	6	8
When cause settled after final hearing, or where Judgment is rendered on such hearing,—			

	£	s.	d.
56. To the Attorney of Plaintiff en faux.	5	16	8
57. To the Attorney of Defendant en faux....	3	10	0
Incidental Cross-demands; one-half of the fees allowed on the original demand,—			

Interventions.

Costs on Interventions to be the same as on Original demands of the same Class.

Oppositions afin de conserver.

If not contested,—

	£	s.	d.
58. If sum due do not exceed £20....	1	5	0
59. If it exceed £20, and do not exceed £50....	2	0	0
60. If it exceed £50, and do not exceed £100....	2	10	0
61. If it exceed £100....	3	0	0

If contested,—

Costs to be the same as in a contested personal action for the same amount, excepting that the costs of any opposition for a sum less than £50, if contested shall be the same as in a contested action of the highest class in the Circuit Court,—

	£	s.	d.
62. Oppositions afin de distraire, afin d'annuller or afin de charge, if not contested....	3	0	0

If contested, costs same as in actions of the second class.

Ratification of Title.

For all proceedings to obtain a Sentence of Ratification of Title,—

	£	s.	d.
63. To the Petitioner's Attorney if purchase money be under £250....	3	10	0
64. If purchase money exceed £250, and do not exceed £500....	5	0	5
65. If purchase money exceed £500....	6	5	0

Fees on Oppositions to sentences of Ratification of Title and upon contestations thereof, to be the same as on Oppositions to Executions and contestations thereof.

Proceedings under 12 Vic., c. 41.

The Costs upon proceedings, under any Writ, (excepting Writs of *Certiorari*) sued out under the provisions of this Statute to be the same as in actions of the third class.

Writs of Certiorari.

	£	s.	d.
If settled before the Motion to file any such Writ,—			
16. To Petitioner	2	6	8
If not settled before such Motion,—			
17. To Petitioner	3	10	0
18. To Respondent	2	10	0

Habeas Corpus.

	£	s.	d.
For all proceedings upon any Writ of Habeas Corpus which shall not be settled before the Motion to file the same,—			
19. To the Petitioner	1	3	4
20. To the Respondent	1	0	0
For the like if settled before the Motion to file the same,—			
21. To the Petitioner	0	13	4
22. To the Respondent	0	11	8

Commission Rogatoire.

	£	s.	d.
23. To the Attornies engaged at the place where the Writ is executed.— To the Attorney prosecuting such Commission	1	3	4
24. To the Respondent	0	11	8
25. For the examination in chief or cross-examination of any witness	0	3	4
26. For all proceedings to obtain Probate of any Will	2	10	0

Evocations.

If the Evocation be maintained, costs to be as in an action of the third class, which costs shall include all service in both Courts,—

	£	s.	d.
77. If Evocation be rejected—To each party	1	3	4

Appeals from Bankrupt Court.

On every contested Appeal which shall be prosecuted to final Judgment, or final hearing,—

	£	s.	d.
78. To Attorney of Appellant	7	10	0
79. To Attorney of Respondent	6	0	0
If Appeal be not contested,—			
80. To Attorney of Appellant	5	16	8
If Appeal be dismissed or settled before final hearing,—			
81. To Attorney of Appellant	3	10	0
82. To Attorney of Respondent	2	6	8

Appeals from Circuit Court.

	If Judgment appealed from amount to £25 or exceed that sum.			If Judgment appealed from do not amount to £25.		
	£	s.	d.	£	s.	d.
On every contested Appeal which shall be prosecuted to final Judgment or hearing,—						
83. To the Attorney for Appellant	3	10	0	2	6	8
84. To the Attorney for Respondent	2	6	8	1	13	4
If Appeal be discontinued or dismissed before final hearing,—						
85. To Appellant	1	15	0	1	3	4
86. To Respondent	1	3	4	0	16	8
If Appeal be not contested,—						
87. To Appellant's Attorney prosecuting Appeal to final Judgment	1	15	0	1	3	4

To the Sheriff for his Fees on the following proceedings, exclusive of disbursements.

	£	s.	d.
88. For a copy of any Writ of Summons addressed to the Sheriff, and Warrant return included......	0	5	0
89. For each additional copy........	0	5	0
90. For all his proceedings on the execution of any *Copias ad respondendum*......	1	0	0
91. For each additional Defendant........	0	10	0
92. For all his proceedings on the execution of any Writ of Attachment or *Saisie arrêt* before Judgment or of any Writ of *Saisie revendication*......	1	0	0
93. For each additional Defendant........	0	5	0
94. For all proceedings on the execution of any Writ of *Saisie Gagerie*......	0	11	8
95. For each additional Defendant......	0	5	0
96. For the return to any Writ issued under the authority of the Provincial Statute, 12, Vic, Cap. 38, sec. 63, and ordered to be returned by the Sheriff into the Superior Court......	0	10	0
97. For all his proceedings on the execution of any Writ of monition......	1	0	0
98. For every additional copy......	0	5	0
99. For the execution of any order for the delivery of goods seized, or for the discharge of a prisoner, return included......	0	3	4
100. For all his proceedings to Summon a Jury under a Writ of *Venire facias*, return included......	1	0	0
101. For his warrant on any Writ of Execution......	0	5	0
102. For each return to any Writ of Execution......	0	5	0
103. On every Opposition filed in his hands, including return......	0	5	0
104. Drawing advertisements for sale of Real Estate under Writ of Execution, copies for Printers, &c......	0	16	8
105. Drawing condition of Sale......	0	6	8
106. For all his proceedings on any Writ of possession......	0	10	0
107. Receiving and enregistering Bond, under 41 Geo. III., c. 7, sec. 15......	0	10	0
108. For every other Bail Bond......	0	5	0
109. Assignment of same, if required......	0	5	0
110. For every Search of Records for one year or less......	0	1	0
111. For every general Search......	0	2	6
112. For every official Certificate......	0	1	0
113. For any Office copy of any document, per hundred words...	0	0	6

No.	Description	£	s	d
114.	For every Deed of Sale of immoveable estate, not exceeding £100, including Registry of Deed.........	1	0	0
115.	For the like, where the consideration exceeds £100.........	1	10	0
116.	For all his proceedings for the arrest of a Defendant under a Writ of *cap. ad. sat.*; or under a Judgment ordering a *contrainte par corps*, including return.........	1	0	0

The above fees to be payable in all cases (excepting when herein otherwise provided for) when the officer is required to perform the duty for which the fee is chargeable.

To the Crier, including the *Tispstaff.*

No.	Description	£	s	d
117.	On the return into Court of any action (this fee to be paid at the time of the return).........	0	3	9
118.	On each contested cause inscribed for *Enquête*.........	0	5	9
119.	On each cause, not contested, inscribed for *Enquête*. (These fees to be paid at the time of the inscription).	0	2	6
120.	In every cause in which a Jury Trial shall be ordered (to be paid at the time of taking out of the *Venire*).........	0	6	8
121.	For all proceedings in a case of *licitation* of one *héritage* or more.........	1	0	0

To the Bailiffs.

No.	Description	£	s	d
122.	For every service of a Writ of Summons and return.........	0	2	0
123.	For every service of a Writ of Subpoena, copy of Judgment, Rule of Court, notice, or other paper, including return.........	0	1	0
124.	For all proceedings on the arrest of any person.........	0	10	0
125.	For all proceedings on any seizure or attachment, including *procès verbal*, not exceeding 300 words.........	0	12	6
126.	For every additional 100 words.........	0	0	4
127.	For every publication in both languages at the Church Door, including *affiches*, affixing same, &c.........	0	2	0
128.	For the sale of goods and chattels.........	0	7	6
129.	For a return of no goods or no lands.........	0	2	6
130.	For a return of *rebellion à Justice*.........	0	5	0

	£	s.	d.
131. For all services executing a Writ of possession......	0	10	0
132. For a *Record*, when required......	0	2	0
133. For attendance on Jury Trials under direction of the Sheriff, per diem......	0	5	0
134. Mileage to be allowed in all cases excepting for the first mile, per league out and in (exclusive of Tolls and Ferries)......	0	1	6

Whenever a Bailiff is the bearer of several Writs to be executed at the same time the charge of mileage to be paid by the Defendants in eq'ial proportions.

In appealable Cases in the Circuit Court, the like fees as above.

QUEBEC, 17th December, 1850.

(Signed,)

EDWD. BOWEN, CHIEF JUSTICE S. C.
D. MONDELET, J. S. C.,
CHS. D. DAY, J. S. C.,
J. SMITH, J. S. C.,
G. VANFELSON, J. S. C.,
CHARLES. MONDELET, J. S. C.,
E. BACQUET, J. S. C.,
J. DUVAL, J. S. C.,
W. C. MEREDITH, J. S. C.

SUPERIOR COURT.

TABLE OF FEES,

OF 1852.

Which abrogates Tariff of December 1850, as to Fees of Attornies and Bailiffs.

LOWER CANADA.—SUPERIOR COURT.

It is hereby ordered, that the following fees be allowed to the Counsel, Advocates and Attornies practising in the Superior Court in actions to be instituted, and upon other proceedings to be commenced from and after the day on which the present Tariff shall be entered by the Prothonotaries of this Court in the Registers of the same as by Law directed; and the Tariff of fees for the Counsel, Advocates and Attornies practising in this Court, the original whereof was entered in the registers of the said Court, at the City of Quebec, on the twenty-first day of December 1850, is hereby repealed in so far as regards actions to be instituted, and other proceedings to be commenced, from and after the day on which the present Tariff shall be so entered in the registers of this Court.

ACTIONS NOT CONTESTED.

	1st CLASS. In personal actions if the matters in contest exceed £100; and in real and mixed actions not otherwise specially provided for; and in actions [en separation de biens,] or [en separation de corps et de biens.		2nd CLASS. In personal actions, if the matters in contest do not exceed £100; and are not otherwise provided for; and in actions [en exhibition de titre,] also in actions [en déclaration de paternité; and upon petitions [en destitution de tutelle] or [de curatelle.	
	Plaintiff's Attorney.	Defendant's Attorney.	Plaintiff's Attorney.	Defendant's Attorney.
	£ s. d.	£ s. d.	£ s. d.	£ s. d.
No. 1. If the action be settled before the Return	4 3 4		3 6 8	
2. If the action be settled, or if Defendant confess judgment, on the day of the return, or on the next following juridical day	5 0 0		4 0 0	

No.		£	s.	d.	£	s.	d.	£	s.	d.	£	s.	d.
3.	If the action be settled, or if Defendant confess judgment, after the delay mentioned in the next preceding number, but before plea filed, or inscription for *Enquête*, or inscription for final hearing on the merits, where no *Enquête* is necessary	5	10	0	4	10	0	5	0	0	2	0	0
4.	If the action be settled after the inscription on the *Roll des Enquêtes*, but before the closing of the *Enquête*, or if the action be settled after the inscription for final hearing on the merits, where no *Enquête* is necessary, or if judgment be rendered on such last mentioned inscription..............		5	0	0		5	0	0					
5.	If the action be settled after *Enquête* closed, or if judgment be rendered in such action after *Enquête*..............	6	5	0	5	16	8	5	0	0	2	6	8
6.	If any of the above cases in which the Defendant may have appeared by Attorney—to Defendant's Attorney..............	7	10	0				7	10	0			

ACTIONS CONTESTED.

No.		£	s.	d.	£	s.	d.	£	s.	d.	£	s.	d.
7.	If the action be settled after the filing of any plea, other than a plea to the merits, and without *Enquête* on such plea, or if the action be dismissed on such plea and without *Enquête*..............	6	5	0		5	0	0		6	5	0	
	If there be an *Enquête* on any such plea, an additional fee of £2 10s. to each Attorney..............												
8.	If the action be settled after the filing of a plea to the merits, but before the inscription on the *Roll des Enquêtes* where an *Enquête* is necessary, or before the inscription for final hearing, where no *Enquête* is necessary..............	8	6	0	6	13	4	6	13	4	8	6	0
9.	If the action be settled after the inscription on the *Roll des Enquêtes*, but before the inscription for final hearing..............	9	7	6	7	10	0	7	10	0	9	7	6
10.	If the action be settled after the inscription for final hearing, or if judgment be rendered on such hearing..............	12	10	0		10	0	0		10	0	0	

a 11 The costs in actions *en revendication* for moveables to be taxed as against the Plaintiff according to the value of the property claimed, and as against the Defendant according to the value of the property for which judgment is rendered. Hypothecary actions and actions for Seigniorial dues where the title of the Seignior is not contested, are to be considered in respect of

12 costs as merely personal actions. The costs in actions *en reddition de compte*, to be taxed as against the Plaintiff, according to the amount demanded, and as against the Defendant, according to the amount for which he is accountable. In any

13 action of ejectment under the lessors and lessees Act. 3, Wm. IV. Chap. 1, the costs to be as in a personal action (in the Superior Court or Circuit Court as the case may be) for a sum of money equal to the rent of the premises leased for the

14 year current at the time of the institution of the action, or if the lease shall have expired, then for the last year the lease

15 extended; save and except cases in which the annual rent shall not exceed £15 in which the costs shall be according to

16 the 3rd class of appealable cases in the Circuit Court. In actions for sums of money, under £50 instituted by writ of *Cap.*

17 *ad resp.* in the Superior Court, the costs to be as in actions in the Circuit Court for like sums, excepting that if the sum for which a writ of *capias ad respondendum* be sued out do not exceed £15 cy. the costs shall be as in an appealable action of the 3rd class in the Circuit Court.

18 In actions of damages for personal wrongs (excepting in actions in which the Court or Jury shall find the damages to be under forty shillings sterling) the costs to be taxed as of the class to be determined by the final judgment.

19 In any case where the Defendants sever in their defence, the Plaintiff's attorney shall receive on each additional issue one half of the sum which he would have received had there been but one issue, the whole amount to be payable in equal

20 proportions by the party or parties to each issue.

Superior Court—Additional Fees.

	£	s.	d.
No. 11. For the second and every additional copy of the Plaintiff's declaration..........	0	5	0
12. Affidavit to obtain *Cap. ad resp* :—*Sa rev* :—*Sa. ar* :—or *Saisie gagerie*, when affidavit required and action commenced by such process..........	0	10	0
13. If a writ of *Capias ad respondendum* or any writ of attachment against moveables be sued out at any time after the institution of the action (affidavit included),— To the Attorney suing out same.......... if action of 1st class.....	3	0	0
if action of 2nd class.....	2	6	8

14. On any exception *déclinatoire, dilatoire* or *péremptoire à la forme,* or *défense au fonds en droit* overruled,—

	£	s.	d.
To the Plaintiff's Attorney	1	10	0
To the Defendant's Attorney	1	3	4

15. On another plea overruled, after law issue raised upon it,—

To the successful party	1	10	0
To the opposite party	1	3	4

16. On any *exception dilatoire* maintained,—

To the Defendant's Attorney	3	10	0
To the Plaintiff's Attorney	2	6	8

The fees allowed in the foregoing Nos. 14 & 16 are exclusive of the fee allowed where an *Enquête* takes place upon any preliminary plea.

17. If the Plaintiff be permitted to amend his declaration after the filing of an *exception à la forme,*—

To the Defendant's Attorney	1	15	0

18. If the Plaintiff be permitted to amend his declaration after the filing of a *défense au fonds en droit,*—

To the Defendant's Attorney	2	6	8

19. For all proceedings on any petition, motion or rule, not specially provided for, upon which costs are ordered to be paid,—

To the party to whom costs are awarded	0	11	8

20. For all proceedings respecting the putting in of security, in any case not otherwise provided for,—

To each Attorney	0	11	6

21. Fee for counsel at *Enquête* in any contested cause whether tried by Jury or not, this fee not to be allowed unless an appearance be filed by the counsel retained,—

	£	s.	d.
To each,........... if action of 1st class.....	2	6	8
if action of 2nd class.....	1	15	0
22. In cases to be tried by Jury,—			
To each Attorney for preparation of factums required by Rule 72,....... if action of 1st. class.....	1	10	0
if action of 2nd class.....	1	0	0
23. On any re-hearing on the merits, ordered in a contested action,—			
To each Attorney........... if action of 1st class.....	2	6	8
if action of 2nd class.....	1	15	0
24. On any re-hearing ordered upon any pleading,—			
To each Attorney...........	1	3	4
25. On any re-hearing ordered upon any rule or other proceeding not specially provided for—			
To each Attorney...........	0	11	8
26. For all proceedings on a *reprise d'instance*, by petition or motion of the *reprenant l'instance,*—			
To the Attorney rept. l'instance...........	2	6	8
To the Attorney of adverse party...........	1	3	4
27. Costs as in the principal action if the *reprise d'instance* be contested, or if it be made by action ; and also on proceedings to have judgment declared executory,—			
28. On every copy of Subpœna certified by the Attorney...........	0	0	6
29. For all proceedings on suing out a Writ of Execution...........	0	6	8
30. For all proceedings on suing out a Writ of *Saisie arrêt* after Judgment,—			
31. If the declaration of the *Tiers Saisie* be not contested,—			
To the Attorney suing out same........... if action of 1st class.....	2	6	8
if action of 2nd class.....	1	15	0

32. For every *Tiers Saisi* above three, 5s. each,—

If contested the costs to be the same as in a contested personal action: the class to be determined by the amount of the judgment against the *Tiers Saisi* if the costs be payable by him; and by the amount claimed by the contestation, if the costs be payable by the party contesting the declaration.

33. For all proceedings for a *contrainte par corps*, or for the imprisonment of any party, or for a Writ of possession, or for an order for a sale in consequence of a *folle enchère*, or for a *scellé*, or for the removal thereof, and for all proceedings on any application either before or after judgment to liberate any person arrested for debt otherwise than by giving bail, or to obtain possession of property seized under mesne process,—

To the Attorney of applicant, if no cause shewn.......... | 1 | 0 | 0 |

if cause shewn but without *Enquête*,—

To the Attorney of applicant.......... | 1 | 10 | 0 |
To the Attorney shewing cause.......... | 1 | 1 | 0 |

34. If an *Enquête* be necessary on any of the proceedings mentionned in the foregoing number or upon any other incidental proceeding not specially provided for,—

To each Attorney an additional Fee of £2 0 0 (to wit, two pounds).

35. For prosecuting to Judgment a report of distribution not contested.......... | 2 | 10 | 0 |

36. For all proceedings upon a contestation of a report of distribution, if the contestation be not withdrawn or acquiesced in, before the inscription for final hearing on the merits, when the amount of the collocation contested is above £100,—

To the Attorney of the party contesting.......... | 4 | 3 | 4 |
To the Attorney of the creditor claiming.......... | 3 | 6 | 8 |

37. If the amount of the collocation contested exceed £50, and do not exceed £100,—

To the Attorney of the party contesting.......... | 3 | 6 | 8 |
To the Attorney of the creditor claiming.......... | 2 | 10 | 0 |

		£	s.	d.
38.	If the amount of the collocation contested, exceed £ 20, and do not exceed £ 50,—			
	To the Attorney of the party contesting	2	10	0
	To the Attorney of the party claiming	2	0	0
39.	If the amount of the collocation contested do not exceed £ 20,—			
	To the Attorney of the party contesting	2	0	0
	To the Attorney of the party claiming	1	10	0
40.	If the contestation be withdrawn or acquiesced in, before the inscription for final hearing on such contestation one half of the above Fees according to the class.			
41.	For all the proceedings after Judgment ordering an account to be rendered in any action *en reddition de compte*, if the account be acquiesced in without *débats*,—			
	To each Attorney	2	6	8
42.	If the account be contested, the costs to be the same as in a contested personal action; the class to be determined by the amount for which the *rendant compte* shall be declared accountable, beyond the amount admitted to be due, by the account filed, if the costs be payable by the *rendant compte*; and by the amount claimed by the *débats de compte*, if the costs be payable by the *ayant compte*.			
43.	In actions *en séparation de biens* or *en séparation de corps et de biens*,—			
	For all proceedings to liquidate the matrimonial rights of the Plaintiff,—			
	If not contested, to Plaintiff's Attorney	2	6	8
	If contested, to each Attorney	5	0	0
44.	For all proceedings to cause a Curator to be appointed to a *délaissement*, in any hypothecary action	1	3	4

And to the Curator £1. 3s. 4d

Interventions, &c.

45. Costs of interventions and incidental cross demands to be the same as on original demands of same class.

Oppositions.

Oppositions *afin de conserver* not contested,—

		£	s.	d.
46.	If the sum do not exceed £20	2	0	0
47.	If it exceed £20, and do not exceed £50	2	6	8
48.	If it exceed £50 and do not exceed £100	2	16	8
49.	If it exceed £100	3	6	8

50. If contested, costs to be same as in a personal action for the same amount in the Superior Court or Circuit Court as the case may be, excepting that the costs upon the contestation of any opposition for a sum not exceeding £15, shall be the same as in contested actions of the *third* class of appealable cases in the Circuit Court.

51. Oppositions *afin de distraire, afin d'annuller*, or *afin de charge*, if not contested ......

52. If contested, costs to be as in actions of the 2nd class ...... £3 6s. 8d.

Ratifications of Title.

For all the proceedings to obtain a sentence of Ratification of Title,—

53. To the petitioner's Attorney if purchase money do not exceed £100 ...... £3 10s. 0d.

	£	s.	d.
54. If purchase money exceed £100, and do not exceed £250, or if the consideration be not of a pecuniary nature......	5	0	0
55. If purchase money exceed £250......	6	5	0
56. Fees on Oppositions to sentence of Ratification of Title and on contestations thereof to be the same as on Oppositions to executions and contestations thereof.			
Proceedings under 12 Vic: C: 41.—			
57. The costs upon proceedings under any writ (excepting writs of certiorari) sued out under this Statute, to be the same as in actions of the 2nd class.			
Writs of Certiorari.			
58. If settled after the motion to file any such writ,—			
To petitioner......	2	6	8
59. If not settled before such motion,—			
To petitioner......	3	10	0
To respondent......	2	10	0
Commissions Rogatoires and Orders for the examination of Witnesses,—			
60. To the Attorney suing out the same......	0	15	0
61. For the drawing of Interrogatories or cross Interrogatories......	1	0	0
To the Attornies engaged where the writ or order, is executed,—			
62. For taking instructions, examining the papers &c. &c. &c., to each......	1	4	4

	£	s.	d.
63. For examining or cross-examining any Witness			
64. To the Attorney prosecuting the execution of the writ or order, an additional Fee of	1	5	0
Probates.			
65. For all Fees to obtain probate of any Will	1	0	0
Evocations.			
66. If the Evocation be maintained, the costs to be the same as in actions of the second class, which costs shall include all services in both Courts,—	2	10	0
67. If evocation be rejected to each Attorney	1	3	4
Appeals from Bankrupt Court,—			
68. On every contested Appeal which shall be prosecuted to final hearing			
To Attorney of Appellant	7	10	0
To Attorney of Respondent	6	0	0
If Appeal be not contested,—			
69. To Attorney of Appellant	5	16	8
If Appeal be dismissed or settled before final hearing—To Attorney of Appellant	3	10	0
To Attorney of Respondent	2	6	8
Appeals from Circuit Court.			
70. If contested—To the Attorney of Appellant	5	0	0
To the Attorney of Respondent	3	0	0
71. If not contested,—To the Attorney of Appellant	3	0	0

72. If appeal be dismissed or settled before final hearing on the merits,—

	£	s.	d.
To the Attorney of Appellant.............	2	10	0
To the Attorney of Respondent.............	1	15	0

Inscriptions en faux.

73. If settled before *moyens de faux* are filed, each motion required by the rules of this Court, and also the declaration to be made by the Defendant *en faux* as to whether he intends to avail himself of the document impeached, shall be taxed as a motion according to the foregoing No. 19.

If settled after the *moyens de faux* are filed, but before the answer, the Fees of the Attorney of the Plaintiff *en faux* shall be as in No. 1, of the Table, and the Fees of the Attorney of the Defendant *en faux* shall be as in No. 6, of the Table, and if the settlement take place at any subsequent stage of the proceedings, or if Judgment be rendered on such inscription *de faux*, the costs shall be as in the original demand, if settled at a like stage.

MONTREAL, 30th June, 1852.

EDWD. BOWEN, CHIEF JUSTICE.
D. MONDELET, J. S. C.
R. H. GAIRDNER, J. S. C.
J. SMITH, J. S. C.
G. VANFELSON,
E. BACQUET, J. C. S.

9 Juillet 1852.

CHARLES MONDELET, J. S. C.
J. DUVAL, J.
W. C. MEREDITH, J. S. C.

Registered and entered at Quebec, this 20th July, 1852.

BURROUGHS & FISET,
Prothy. S. C.

SUPERIOR COURT.

TABLE OF

ADDITIONAL FEES.

LOWER CANADA.—SUPERIOR COURT.

It is ordered that the following fees be allowed to the Bailiffs of this Court for services to be performed from and after the day on which the present Tariff shall be entered by the Prothonotaries of this Court in the Registers of the same as by law required; and the Tariff of Fees for the Bailiffs of this Court, the original whereof was entered in the Register of the said Court, at the City of Quebec, on the twenty-first day of December, 1850, is hereby repealed in so far as regards services to be performed by the Bailiffs of this Court from and after the day on which the present Tariff shall be so entered in the Registers of this Court.

To the Bailiffs.

	£	s.	d.
For the service of any notice or other paper, upon an Attorney as such, including return........	0	1	0
For the service of a Writ of a Subpœna on each witness, including return........	0	1	6
For the service of any Writ of Summons or other writ or paper not otherwise provided for including return....	0	2	0
For the service of any Writ or other document required by law to be served personally, including return....	0	2	6
For all proceedings on the arrest of any person, including return when required....	0	10	0
For the seizure of Real Estate, or the seizure or attachment of moveables, including original *procès verbal* and copies for the *Saisi* and for the guardian to moveables........	0	12	6
If more than one lot of land included in any seizure, for each additional lot....	0	2	6
For every publication in both languages at the Church door, not otherwise provided for including *affiches* affixing same, &c....	0	2	6
For the sale of real or personal property, including *procès verbal* of sale, and copy....	0	10	0
If more than one lot of land be sold under the same Writ, for each additional lot sold....	0	2	6
For a *procès verbal* of no goods or no lands including copy, if required....	0	2	6
For a *procès verbal* of *Rébellion à Justice* and copy....	0	5	0
For all services executing a Writ of possession, including *procès verbal*....	0	10	0
For *Recors* when required....	0	2	6

	£	s.	d.
If *Recors* necessarily employed more than half a day at the rate of 3s. 4d. per day			
For the appointing of a new guardian when legally required so to do, including procès verbal, copy &c......	0	5	0
For the posting and publication of Exparte Notices for a Ratification of Title, including return, &c......	1	0	0
For the attendance on Jury Trials under the direction of the Sheriff *per diem* (when required)......	0	5	0
In any case in which in consequence of more than one person being interested in the property seized or sold an additional Copy or Copies of a *procès verbal* is or are necessary for each extra Copy so required......	0	2	6
If in consequence of the quantity of goods to be seized or sold, a Bailiff is necessarily occupied more than one day, in making such Seizure or Sale, the additional time when certified by the Sheriff, to be charged at the rate of 10s. per day......	0	10	0

If any paper to be prepared by a Bailiff excepting *procès verbaux* of seizure of real estate, necessarily contains more than 300 words, the additional words to be charged at the rate of four pence per 100 words, in addition to the fees hereinbefore allowed.

Mileage on the Service or Execution of a Writ or of Process of a kind, at the rate of one shilling per mile as heretofore, without any further charge for mileage on any other process to be served on the same party then in the hands of the Bailiff, and which shall be or might have been served at the same time, (whether such process shall have been sued out by the same party or by any other,) and without any charge for mileage in returning, but exclusive of sums paid at Tollgates, Ferries and Bridges. No mileage to be allowed, unless the distance exceed one mile.

MONTREAL, 30th June 1852.

EDWD. BOWEN, Chief Justice.
D. MONDELET, J. S. C.
R. H. GAIRDNER, J. S. C.
J. SMITH, J. S. C.
G. VANFELSON,
E. BACQUET, J C. S.

9 Juillet 1852.

CHARLES. MONDELET, J. S. C.
J. DUVAL, J. S. C.
W. C. MEREDITH, J. S. C.

Registered and entered at Quebec, this 20th July 1852.

BURROUGHS & FISET, Prothy. S. C.

IT IS ORDERED that the following Fees be allowed to the Attornies practising in the SUPERIOR COURT, and to the other Officers hereinafter named.

	£	s.	d.
1. For any Statement (*articulation*) of Facts...	1	10	0
2. For the Answer thereto...	1	0	0
3. When the *Enquête* in any contested case shall be continued in consequence of the party bound to proceed not being ready—to the adverse party...	0	10	0
4. It is ordered that the Attorney's Fee taxable in each of the cases specified in the 75th and 78th Sections of the Judicature Act shall be...	2	0	0

Fees of Commissaires Enquêteurs.

	£	s.	d.
5. Upon every case referred to him... Which said Fee shall be deposited in the hands of the Prothonotary at the time of making the motion of reference to the *Commissaire Enquêteur*.	2	0	0
6. For every witness over six, examined in any case... Which said last mentioned Fee shall be paid to the Commissioner before the inscription of the cause for hearing on the merits, and his certificate of such payment shall be filed of record before the hearing of the case.	0	5	0

The Fees so paid shall form part of the costs to be taxed against the party who by the final Judgment shall be made liable to pay the same.

Montreal, 24th December 1857.

EDWD. BOWEN, CHIEF JUSTICE S. C.

W. C. MEREDITH, J. S. C.   CHS. D. DAY, J. S. C.
A. N. MORIN, J. C. S.   J. SMITH, J. S. C.
J. CHABOT, J. C. S.   CHARLES MONDELET, J. S. C.
J. C. BRUNEAU, J. S. C.   W. BADGLEY, J. S. C.
J. S. McCORD, J. S. C.   W. POWER, J. S. C.

Registered and entered at Quebec, this 4th January, 1858.

BURROUGHS & FISET, P. S. C.

THE Justices of His Majesty's Court of King's Bench for the District of Quebec, having taken into their consideration the Table of Fees which is allowed to the different Officers of the said Court by the Order of the first day of June, 1810, (" until upon further consideration and experience the same should be altered,") and the representations as to the said Table of Fees, which from time to time have been made and submitted by the different officers of the said Court—

It is hereby ordered as follows :—

That in all cases to be instituted, (from and after the first day of January next,) the following table of Fees be allowed to the Prothonotary in lieu of the Tables of Fees fixed and established by the Order of this Court of the said first day of June, 1810, that is to say—

Fees to the Prothonotary in the Superior Term.

	£	s.	d.
That upon every contested cause there be allowed to the Prothonotary a fee of 30s. to be paid as follows :			
By the Plaintiff on the entry and calling of the cause	1	0	0
By the Defendant at the time of his filing any plea or pleas either to the instance or to the action, (except a confession of Judgment, upon which no fee shall be allowed)	0	10	0
And when two or more Defendants shall sever in their defence, each Defendant shall pay the same fee of 10s.	0	10	0
That in default cases, the Prothonotary's fee shall be 20s. payable by the Plaintiff as above	1	0	0
For each and every Writ, the Writ of Subpœna alone excepted	0	3	0
For every Writ of Subpœna wherein shall not be inserted the names of more than four Witnesses	0	1	0
And for each Copy if required	0	0	6
For each and every Office Copy of a Judgment not exceeding 100 words	0	2	0
And for every additional 100 words	0	0	6
For each and every Office Copy of a Rule of Court	0	1	0
For each and Every Office Certificate	0	1	0
For a search beyond a year from the period of making the search	0	1	0
No allowance is made to the Prothonotary for a search within the year reckoning as above, nor for a search upon issuing any Writ of Execution.			

	£	s.	d.
For every recognizance or Bail Bond taken in or out of Court............	0	2	0
For a *Projet de Distribution* or Collocation where the Creditors collocated do not exceed four in number, exclusive of the Attornies and Officers of the Court, if the *Projet* be homologated............	0	13	4
For the like between more than four Creditors, exclusive of the Attornies and Officers of the Court, if the *Projet* be homologated............	1	3	4
Upon Oppositions *afin de distraire, afin d'annuller, afin de charge,* or *afin de conserver* and upon every *Inscription en faux,* or Incidental demand, there shall be allowed to the Prothonotary the same fee as upon causes in chief payable in the same manner.			
It being provided that upon any Opposition *afin d'annuller, afin de charge, afin de distraire,* or *afin de conserver,* which shall not be contested, the Prothonotary shall be entitled to 10s. and no more and shall refund 10s. to the Opposant out of the 20s. which shall have been paid by the Opposant on, or before the return day of the Writ of Execution............	0	10	0
Upon every Opposition *afin de conserver* which shall be contested, there shall be paid to the Prothonotary by the party contesting the same, at the time of filing his plea of contestation a sum of 10s............	0	10	0
For all Fees on a Contestation of a Report of Distribution or Collocation 5s. to be paid by the party contesting at the time of the filing the contestation............	0	5	0
If any answer be put into the contestation, the fee of the Prothonotary thereon shall be 5s. to be paid by the party filing the answer at the time of the filing of the same............	0	5	0
For the execution of a Commission *Rogatoire* 5s............	0	5	0
For every Deposition taken in virtue of such Commission 3s............	0	3	0
For a Commission *Rogatoire,* or Commission in the nature of a Commission *Rogatoire,* including all the necessary forms to be annexed thereto............	0	5	0
For all the Prothonotary's services in relation to a Writ of *Certiorari* Attachment or *Habeas Corpus, which* shall not be settled before filing the same............	0	10	0
For all the Prothonotary's services on a Writ of Error, Prohibition *Mandamus* or *quo-Waranto* which all not be settled before the filing thereof............	1	0	0
For preparing a List of Jurors............	0	2	6
For attendance and striking a Jury............	0	2	6
For publication of a Will or Act containing a substitution or *Fedei Commis*............	0	11	8

For registering the same at the rate of 6d. per each and every hundred words.

The like fees upon the probate of a last Will and Testament.

	£	s.	d.
For all this fees upon a Licitation of one heritage 20s. to be paid by the *poursuivant* 6s. 8d. previous to the first *crié*, 6s. 8d. previous to the second *crié*, and 6s. 8d. previous to the third *crié*	1	0	0
For each and every additional *héritage* included in such licitation, the Prothonotary shall be entitled to an additional fee of 5s. to be paid in the same manner and in the same proportion as above	0	5	0
For affixing and taking off seals of safe custody (*scellé*,) the Prothonotary or Commissioner shall be entitled to a fee of 7s. 6d. for each and every vacation not exceeding two vacations	0	7	6
Vacations per diem to be paid by the *poursuivant* previous to the closing of each vacation.			
For every copy of any paper in his custody, the Prothonotary shall be allowed 2s. for the first two hundred words, and 6d. for each and every additional 100 words including Certificate	0	2	0
For his fee on making up a Record on a Writ of Appeal and returning the Writ 13s. 4d. exclusive of transcript to be paid for as a Copy under this Tariff	0	13	4
For every *Acte of Avis de Parents*, including the order for convening the *assemblée* and Copy of the *Acte*	0	3	0
Upon an *Avis de Parents* taken in the country parts by a Sub-delegate including the *Acte* of homologation and Copy the Prothonotary shall be entitled to receive 3s.	0	3	0
For every attendance out of his office the Prothonotary shall be entitled to receive 7s. 6d. for each Vacation, not exceeding two Vacations per diem exclusive of travelling expences	0	7	6
For a *Clôture d'Inventaire*	0	3	0
For all services on the application of a candidate to be examined in order to his being commissioned as an Advocate or as a Notary	0	6	8
For the safe-keeping and payment of all monies deposited with the Prothonotaries, they shall be entitled to retain at the rate of 20s. on the first £100 and of 10s. upon each and every additional £100, and in that proportion upon any lesser sum.			
For enregistering a renunciation to a community or succession or donation, or any other document to be enregistered	0	0	6
for every hundred words 6d.			
For every Evocation from the Inferior Term when the Evocation is dismissed	0	6	8

Quebec, 20th October 1830.

J. SEWELL, Chief Justice.
J. KERR, J. B. R.
EDWD. BOWEN, J. B. R.
J. T. TASCHEREAU, J. B. R.

LOWER CANADA.—COURT OF APPEALS.

WEDNESDAY, 10th March 1847.

PRESENT:

THE HONORABLE SIR JAMES STUART, BART., C. J.
   " MR. JUSTICE BOWEN,
   " MR. JUSTICE ROLLAND,
   " MR. JUSTICE PANET,
   " MR. JUSTICE DAY.

IT IS ORDERED by the Court of Appeals now here, in pursuance of the authority in them vested by the Statute in such case made and provided, that there shall be allowed to the Prothonotary of the Court of Queen's Bench, for the District of Quebec, the following Fees for the services herein after mentioned, that is to say :—

	£	s.	d.
For taking each and every deposition beyond the number of four depositions, in every cause, in which four depositions shall be taken, for each, the sum of............................	0	2	0
Secondly.—For the services of the Prothonotary on all motions and rules for attachment, and incidental proceedings, the sum of............	0	13	4
Thirdly.—For the services of the Prothonotary on all motions or rules for sales at the *folle enchère* of the Purchaser, and all incidental proceedings, the sum of............	0	13	4
Fourthly.—For all motions or rules at the instance of Purchasers, to be permitted to retain the purchase money or part thereof and all incidental proceedings, the sum of............	0	13	4
Fifthly.—For the services of the Prothonotary on all motions for one of the Prerogative Writs of the Crown, and all incidental proceedings, the sum of............	0	13	4

Certified,

JOHN VON EXTER, Deputy C. C. A.